THE
CHRISTMAS
PIÑATA

JACK
KENT

Parents' Magazine Press · New York

Library of Congress Cataloging in Publication Data

Kent, Jack
   The Christmas piñata.
   SUMMARY. Considered useless by the potter and his
family because it is cracked, a little pot becomes
the center of attention when it is chosen to make a
Christmas piñata.
   [1. Christmas—Fiction] I. Title.
PZ7.K414Ch   [E]   74-30450
ISBN 0-8193-0815-3   ISBN 0-8193-0816-1 lib. bdg.

They were just two lumps
of clay to begin with.
But in the talented hands
of Juan Gomez, the potter,
they began to take shape.

Soon they were two
handsome pots. Just alike.

Pedro Gomez helped his father put the pots into the oven to be baked hard and strong. But when they took them out again they saw that one of them had cracked.

"Well," sighed Señor Gomez, "that's one pot that won't go to market!" And he shoved it into a corner out of the way.

Poor little pot. If it had a heart, that would be broken, too.

It watched with envy as Señor Gomez painted
the rest of the pottery with gay shapes
and bright colors.

"How pretty the other pot is," thought the broken pot. And it sighed a great sigh. "No one would decorate a broken pot like me!"

Saturday was market day.
Pedro helped his father carry
the pottery into town.

The broken pot sadly watched them go.

But the good pot didn't go to market either. Señora Gomez said it was just what she needed for carrying water from the well.

"How useful the other pot is," thought the broken pot. And it sighed another great sigh. "No one has any use for a broken pot like me!"

Days passed. The broken pot sat in the corner. Forgotten.

Then, one day, Maria Gomez noticed the pot and said, "Look, Mama! It's just what we need for our Christmas piñata!"
"I'm needed!" the broken pot said happily to itself.

"What sort of piñata shall it be?"
Señora Gomez asked. "Last year it
was a star. And the year before
that a burro."

"Let's make a bull this time," said Maria.

Using the pot for the body, Maria and her mother added legs and a neck of sticks tied with string.

"It's dark in here!" thought the pot, as
it was covered with a skin of torn-up
newspapers soaked in flour paste.
Slowly the form of a bull began to take shape.

Then it was covered with fringed strips
of colored tissue paper.
"It's beautiful!" said Maria.
"I'm beautiful!" the proud pot said
happily to itself.

Maria cut a slit in the bull's back,
just over the mouth of the pot. Then
she and her mother filled the pot with
candies and fruits and nuts and other
good things.

The piñata was ready.

Christmas drew near. In front of the Gomez house
the decorations were hung. And proudly among
them, its outside covered with tissue paper
and its inside filled with treats, hung the broken pot.

One night, candles could be seen flickering
in the dark. It was the traditional
Christmas celebration, Las Posadas.

In Las Posadas the children were acting
out the search for shelter on that night
in Bethlehem long ago. From house to
house they went, but at each they were
told there was no room.

Until at last, at the Gomez house, they
were told they could stay.
"I'm glad!" the pot said to itself.

Then there was great joy, and everyone joined in singing the happy songs of Christmas.

After a while Señora Gomez said, "It's time for the piñata."

"That's ME!" thought the pot. And it felt terribly important.

Maria was blindfolded and handed a stick.

She began thrashing about and several times came very close to the piñata. "If she's not careful she's going to *hit* me!" thought the pot.

That was the whole idea, of course, and the children took turns trying.

Finally one of them hit the piñata and shattered
the pot. Good things rained down and the children
scrambled for them, squealing with delight.

U.S. 1878006

The piñata was a shambles. And the pot was smashed to bits.
"Well," thought the bits as they were tossed onto the trash heap, "it was grand while it lasted."

After a long while, or a short while,
the bits of the broken pot were joined
by the bits of the good pot.

"Did you get broken, too?" the bits
of the broken pot asked in surprise.
"Nothing lasts forever," the bits of
the good pot replied.

"We began the same and we ended the same," said
one pile of bits.
"Everybody does," said the other.
"And in between, we were each useful in our own
way," said one.
"Everybody is," said the other.

And the whole trash heap sighed happily.
For there is contentment in knowing that
whoever you are, you're somebody.